W9-BXC-106

young
justice ™

1

STONE ARCH BOOKS
a capstone imprint

young Justice™

AQUALAD

AGE: 16   SECRET IDENTITY: Kaldur' Ahm

BIO: Aquaman's apprentice; a cool, calm warrior and leader;
totally amphibious with the ability to bend and shape water.

SUPERBOY

AGE: 16   SECRET IDENTITY: Conner Kent

BIO: Cloned from Superman; a shy and uncertain teenager;
gifted with super-strength, infrared vision, and leaping abilities.

ARTEMIS

AGE: 15   SECRET IDENTITY: Classified

BIO: Green Arrow's niece; a dedicated and tough fighter;
extremely talented in both archery and martial arts.

KID FLASH

AGE: 15   SECRET IDENTITY: Wally West

BIO: Partner of the Flash; a competitive team member, often
lacking self-control; gifted with super-speed.

ROBIN

AGE: 13   SECRET IDENTITY: Dick Grayson

BIO: Partner of Batman; the youngest member of the team;
talented acrobat, martial artist, and hacker.

MISS MARTIAN

AGE: 16   SECRET IDENTITY: M'gann M'orzz

BIO: Martian Manhunter's niece; polite and sweet; ability to
shape-shift, read minds, transform, and fly.

THE STORY SO FAR...

The Justice League of America sanctions a new group of teenage super heroes. Young Justice,
under the guidance of the JLA, will perform covert operations in the fight against evil. But first,
the team will have to adjust to their new headquarters and a new member...

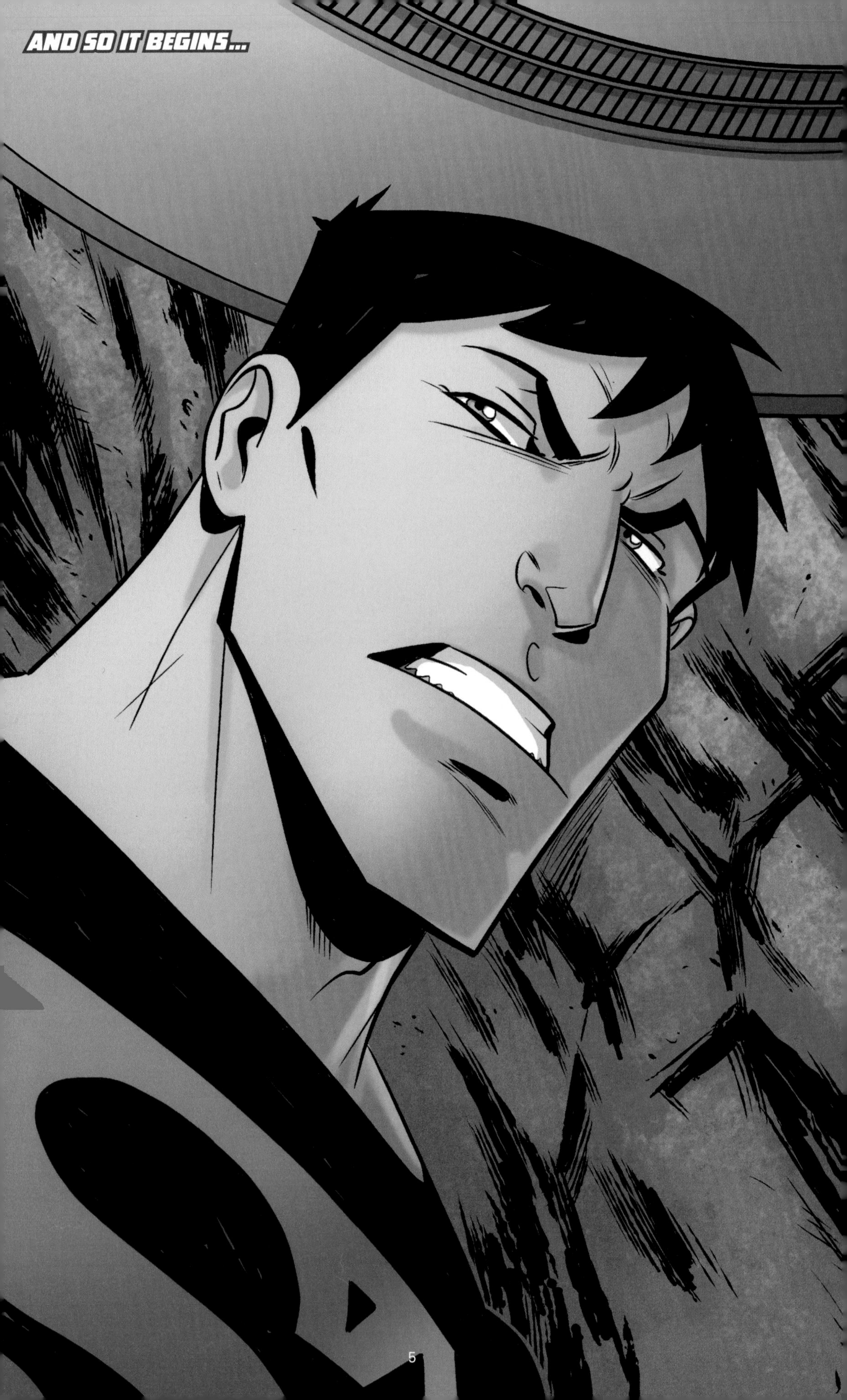
AND SO IT BEGINS...

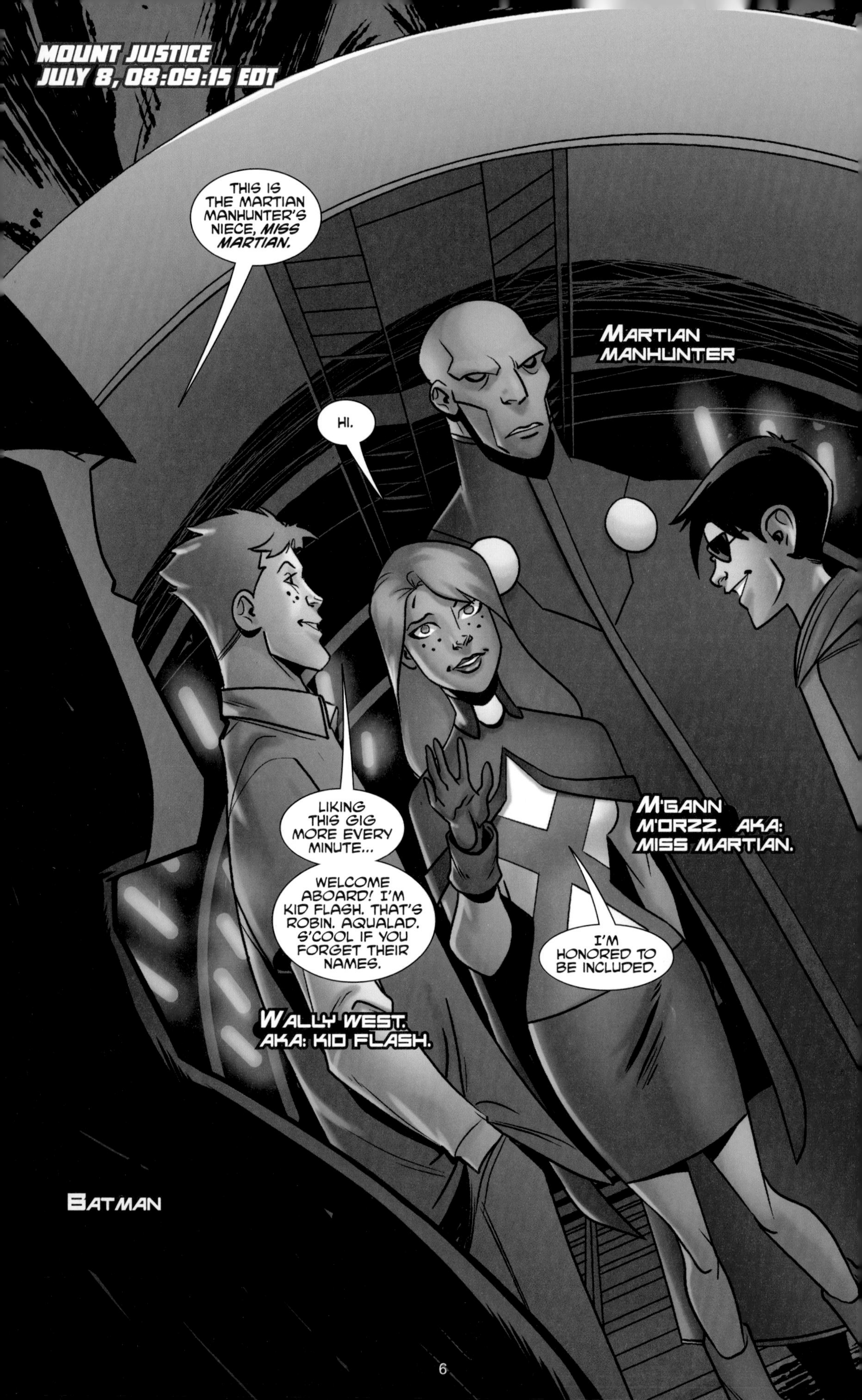
MOUNT JUSTICE
JULY 8, 08:09:15 EDT
THIS IS THE MARTIAN MANHUNTER'S NIECE, MISS MARTIAN.
MARTIAN MANHUNTER
HI.
LIKING THIS GIG MORE EVERY MINUTE...
WELCOME ABOARD! I'M KID FLASH. THAT'S ROBIN. AQUALAD. S'COOL IF YOU FORGET THEIR NAMES.
M'GANN M'ORZZ. AKA: MISS MARTIAN.
I'M HONORED TO BE INCLUDED.
WALLY WEST. AKA: KID FLASH.
BATMAN

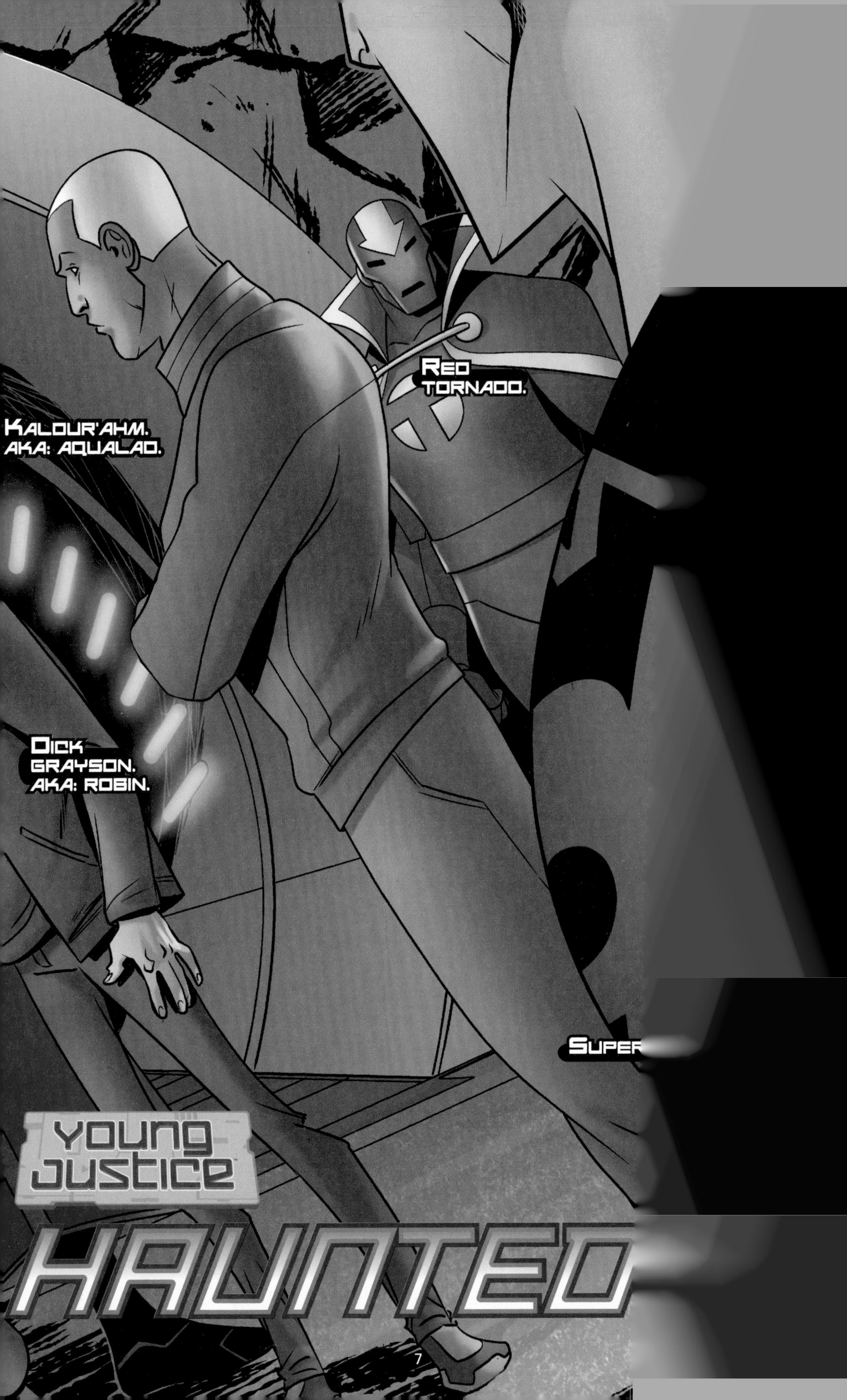

KALDUR'AHM.
AKA: AQUALAD.
RED
TORNADO.
DICK
GRAYSON.
AKA: ROBIN.
YOUNG
JUSTICE
HAUNTED

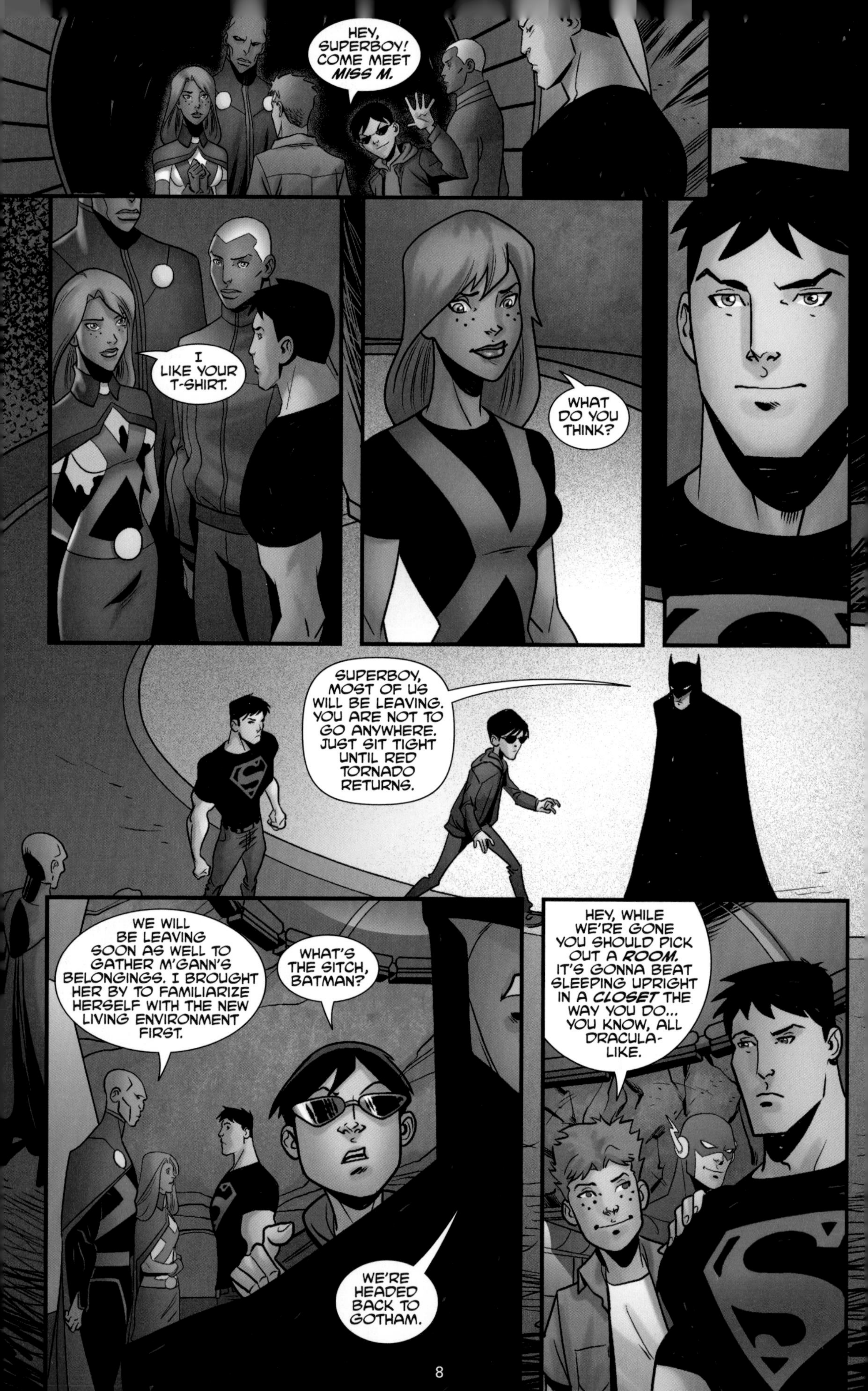
HEY, SUPERBOY! COME MEET MISS M.
I LIKE YOUR T-SHIRT.
WHAT DO YOU THINK?
SUPERBOY, MOST OF US WILL BE LEAVING. YOU ARE NOT TO GO ANYWHERE. JUST SIT TIGHT UNTIL RED TORNADO RETURNS.
WE WILL BE LEAVING SOON AS WELL TO GATHER M'GANN'S BELONGINGS. I BROUGHT HER BY TO FAMILIARIZE HERSELF WITH THE NEW LIVING ENVIRONMENT FIRST.
WHAT'S THE SITCH, BATMAN?
WE'RE HEADED BACK TO GOTHAM.
HEY, WHILE WE'RE GONE YOU SHOULD PICK OUT A ROOM. IT'S GONNA BEAT SLEEPING UPRIGHT IN A CLOSET THE WAY YOU DO... YOU KNOW, ALL DRACULA-LIKE.

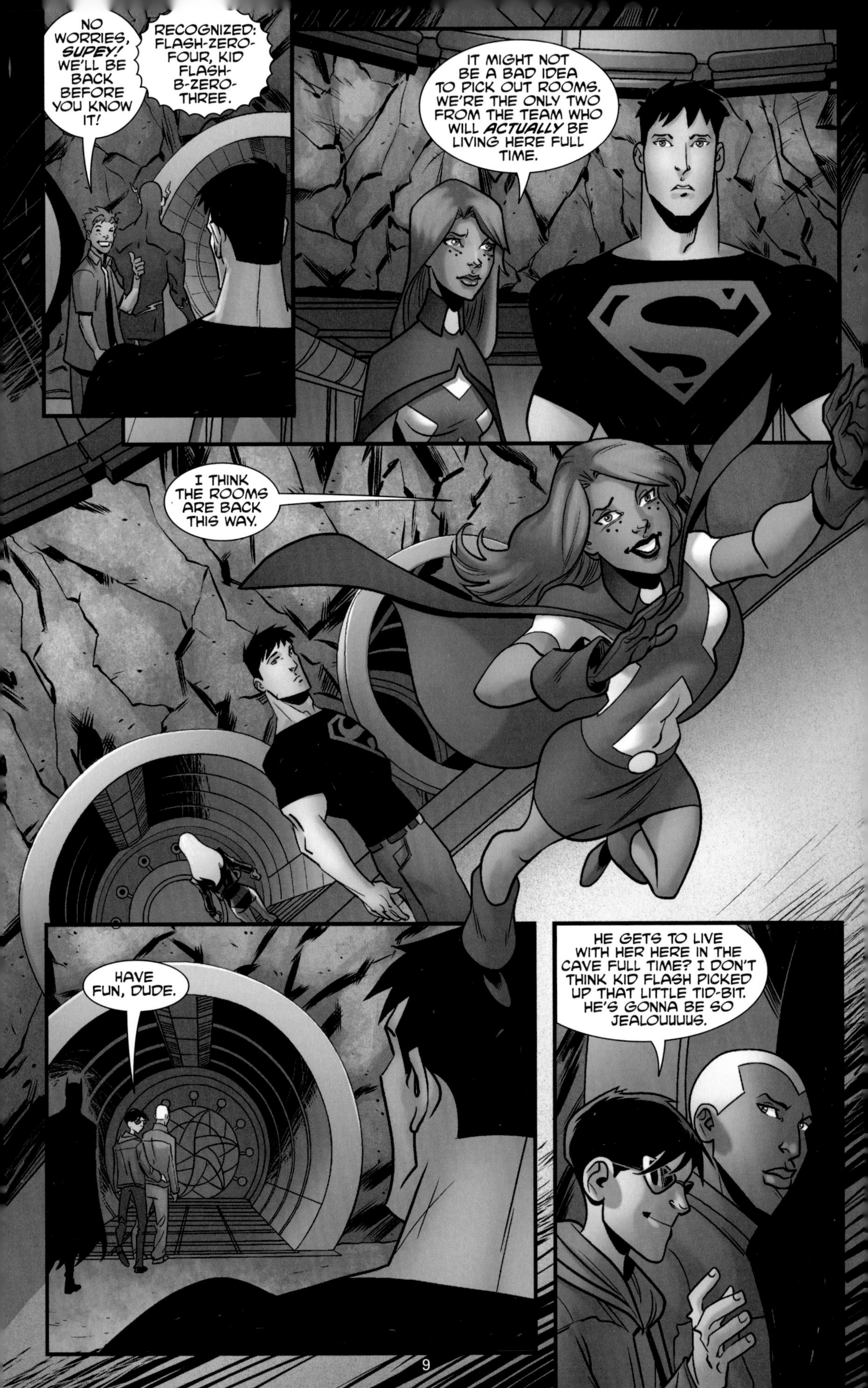
NO WORRIES, SUPEY! WE'LL BE BACK BEFORE YOU KNOW IT!
RECOGNIZED: FLASH-ZERO-FOUR, KID FLASH-B-ZERO-THREE.
IT MIGHT NOT BE A BAD IDEA TO PICK OUT ROOMS. WE'RE THE ONLY TWO FROM THE TEAM WHO WILL ACTUALLY BE LIVING HERE FULL TIME.
I THINK THE ROOMS ARE BACK THIS WAY.
HAVE FUN, DUDE.
HE GETS TO LIVE WITH HER HERE IN THE CAVE FULL TIME? I DON'T THINK KID FLASH PICKED UP THAT LITTLE TID-BIT. HE'S GONNA BE SO JEALOUUUUS.

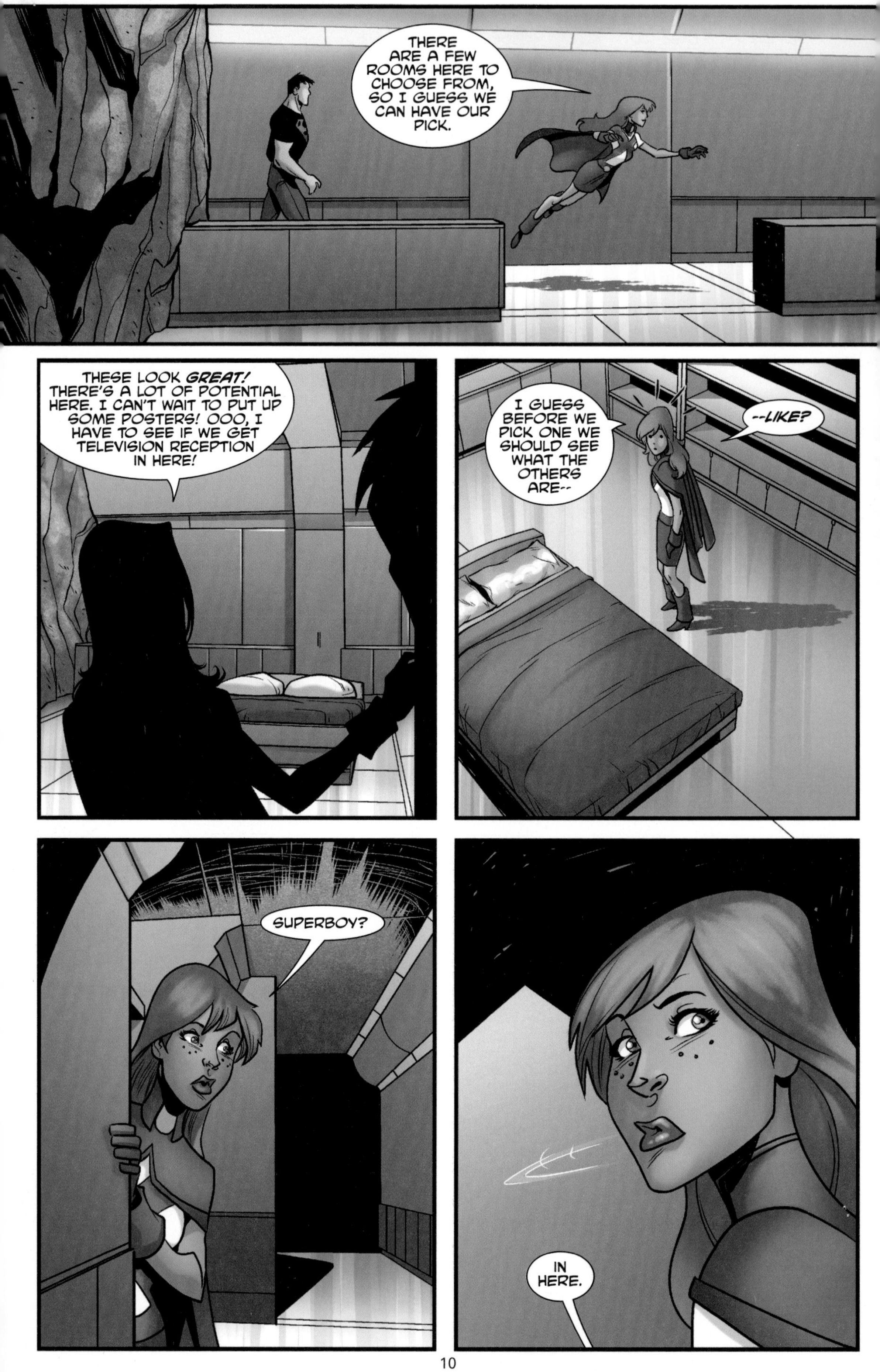
THERE ARE A FEW ROOMS HERE TO CHOOSE FROM, SO I GUESS WE CAN HAVE OUR PICK.
THESE LOOK GREAT! THERE'S A LOT OF POTENTIAL HERE. I CAN'T WAIT TO PUT UP SOME POSTERS! OOO, I HAVE TO SEE IF WE GET TELEVISION RECEPTION IN HERE!
I GUESS BEFORE WE PICK ONE WE SHOULD SEE WHAT THE OTHERS ARE--
--LIKE?
SUPERBOY?
IN HERE.

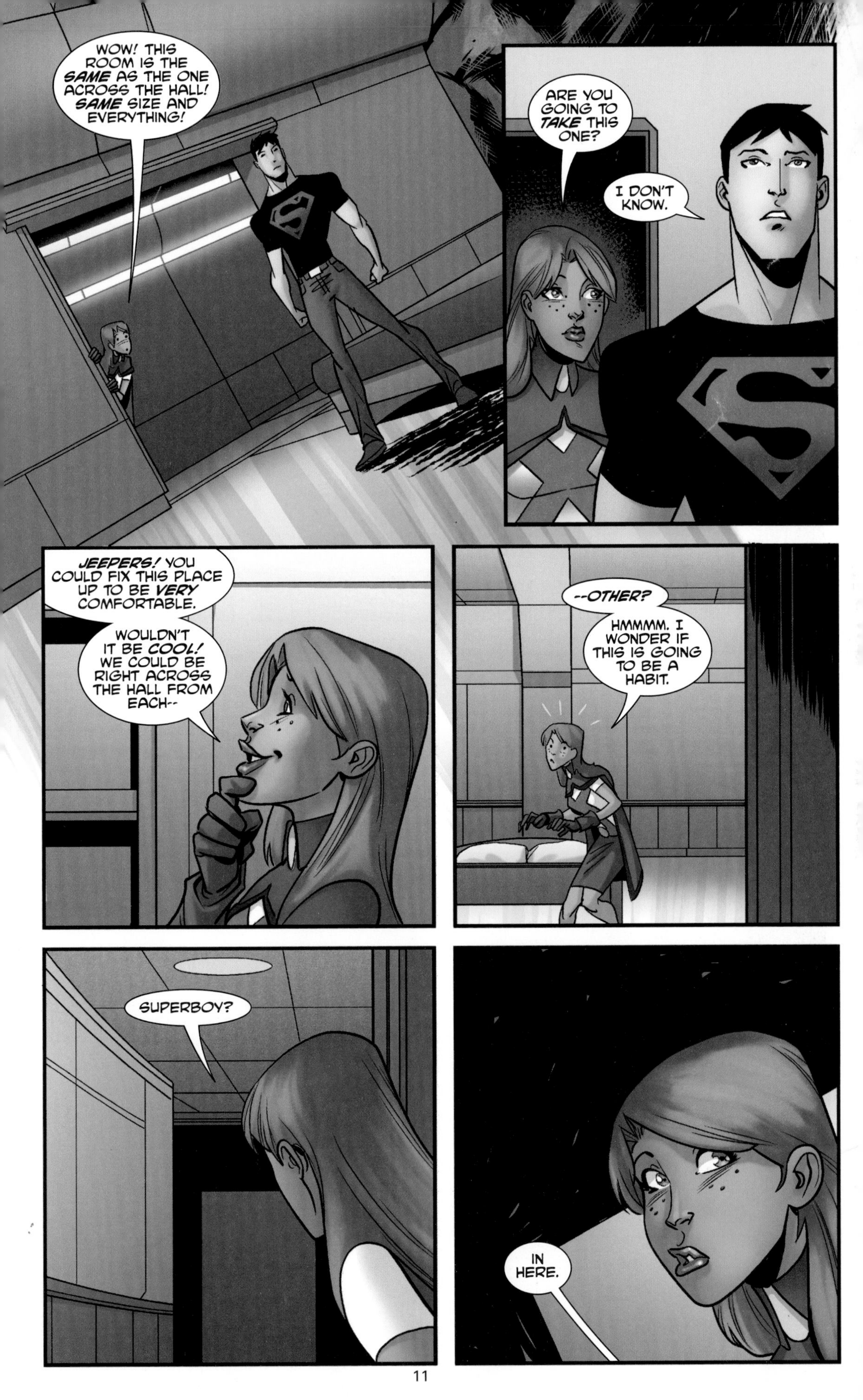
WOW! THIS ROOM IS THE SAME AS THE ONE ACROSS THE HALL! SAME SIZE AND EVERYTHING!
ARE YOU GOING TO TAKE THIS ONE?
I DON'T KNOW.
JEEPERS! YOU COULD FIX THIS PLACE UP TO BE VERY COMFORTABLE.
WOULDN'T IT BE COOL! WE COULD BE RIGHT ACROSS THE HALL FROM EACH--
--OTHER?
HMMMM. I WONDER IF THIS IS GOING TO BE A HABIT.
SUPERBOY?
IN HERE.

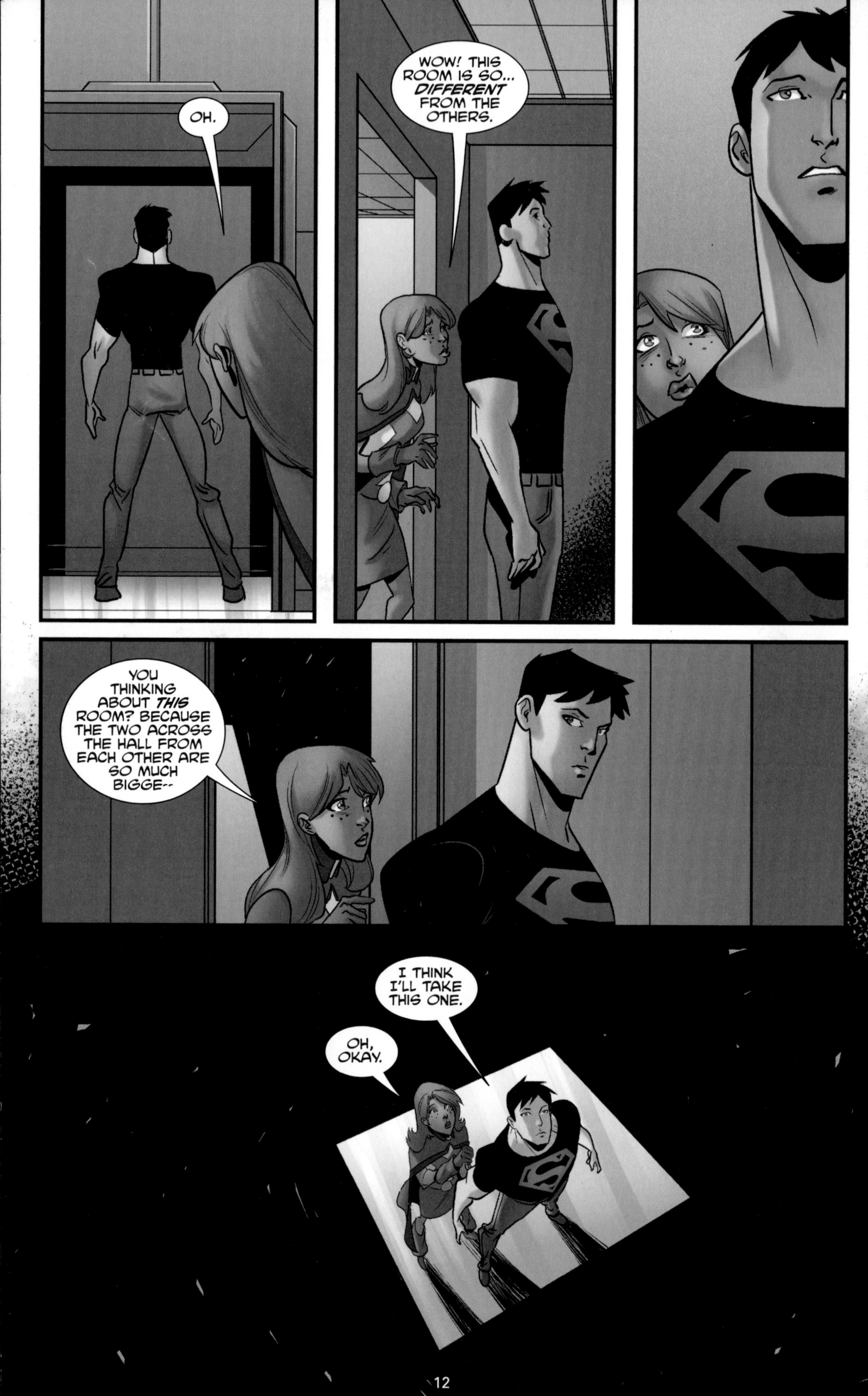
OH.
WOW! THIS ROOM IS SO... *DIFFERENT* FROM THE OTHERS.
YOU THINKING ABOUT *THIS* ROOM? BECAUSE THE TWO ACROSS THE HALL FROM EACH OTHER ARE SO MUCH BIGGE--
I THINK I'LL TAKE THIS ONE.
OH, OKAY.

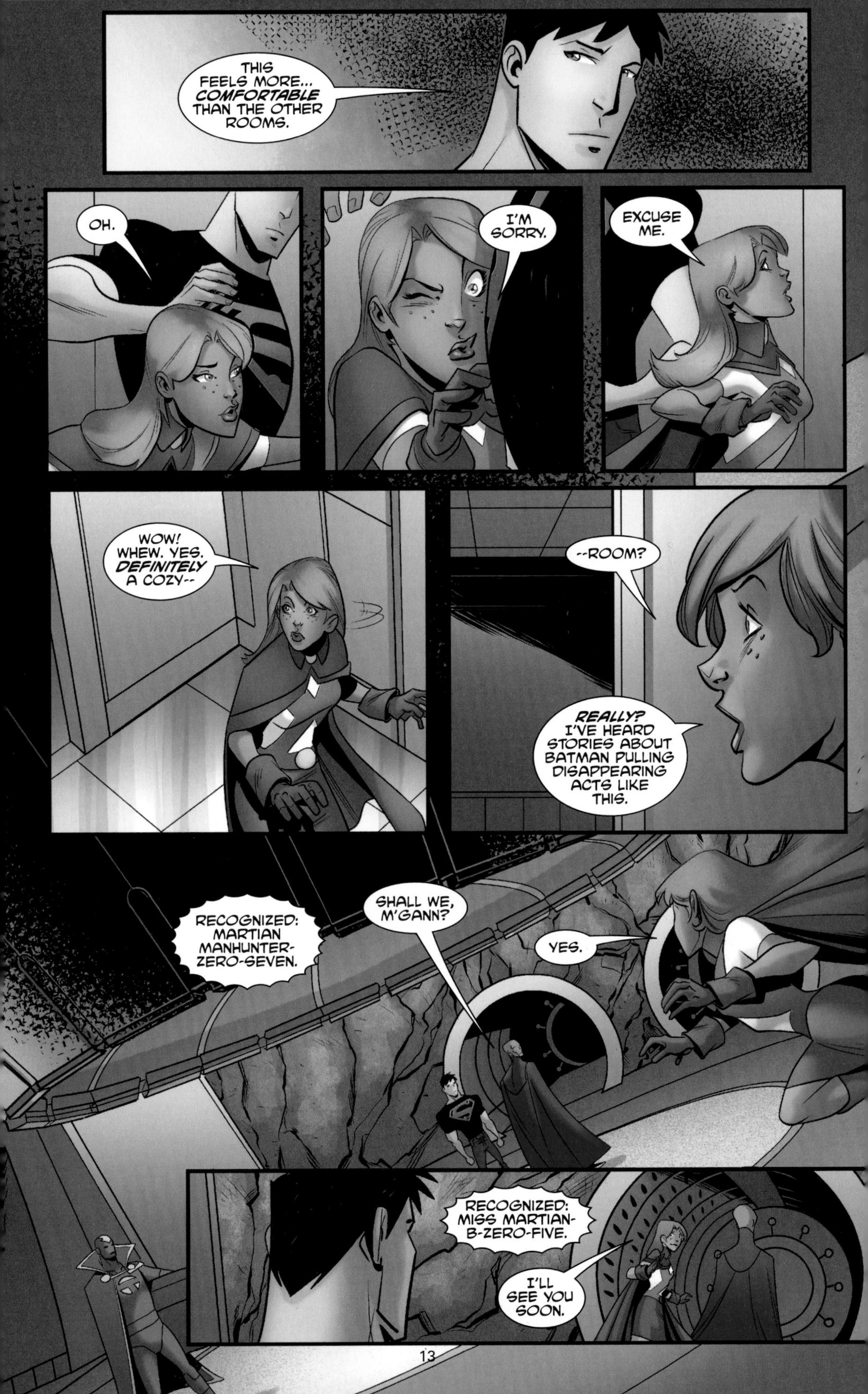
THIS FEELS MORE... COMFORTABLE THAN THE OTHER ROOMS.
OH.
I'M SORRY.
EXCUSE ME.
WOW! WHEW. YES. DEFINITELY A COZY--
--ROOM?
REALLY? I'VE HEARD STORIES ABOUT BATMAN PULLING DISAPPEARING ACTS LIKE THIS.
RECOGNIZED: MARTIAN MANHUNTER-ZERO-SEVEN.
SHALL WE, M'GANN?
YES.
RECOGNIZED: MISS MARTIAN-B-ZERO-FIVE.
I'LL SEE YOU SOON.

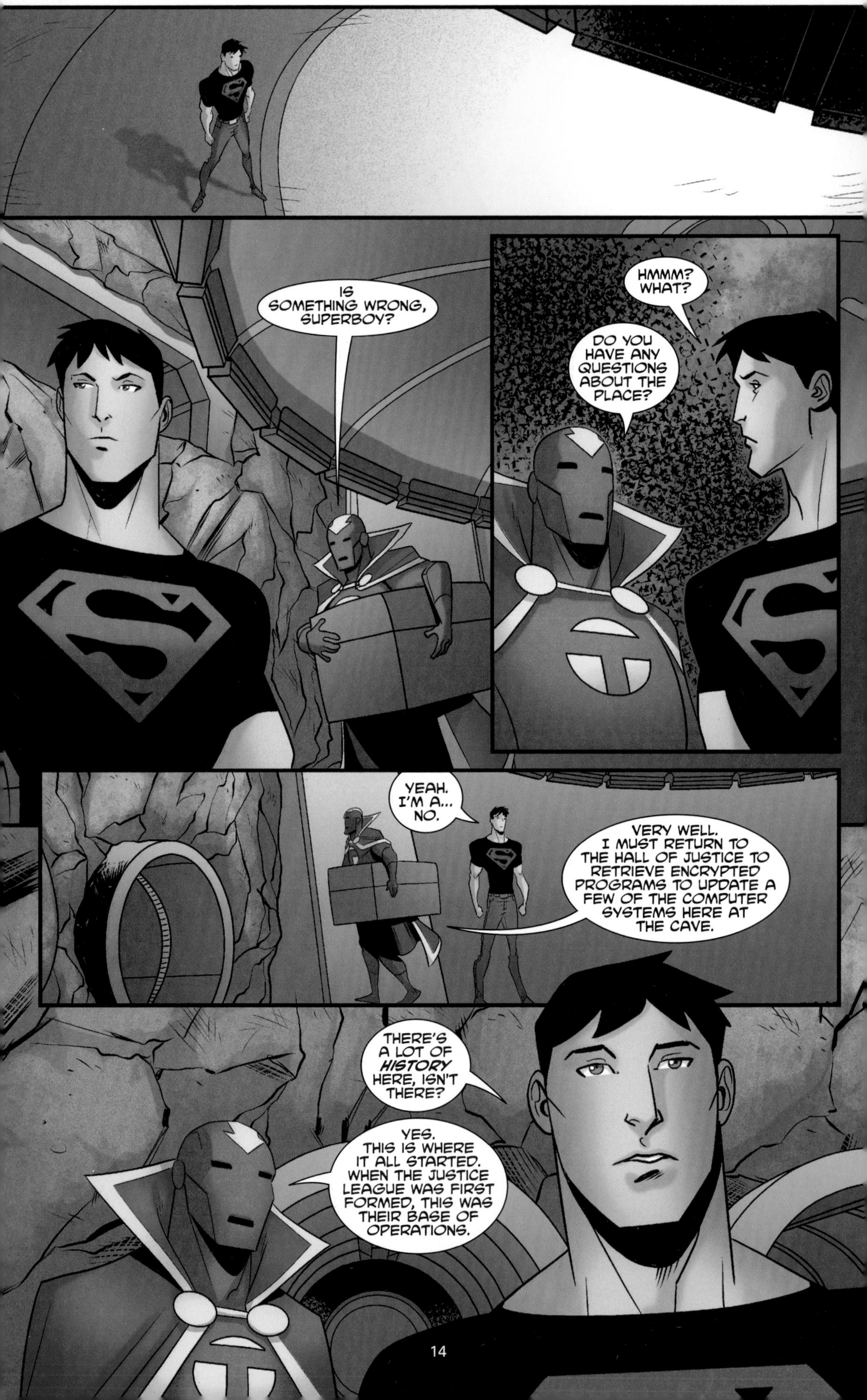
IS SOMETHING WRONG, SUPERBOY?
HMMM? WHAT?
DO YOU HAVE ANY QUESTIONS ABOUT THE PLACE?
YEAH. I'M A... NO.
VERY WELL. I MUST RETURN TO THE HALL OF JUSTICE TO RETRIEVE ENCRYPTED PROGRAMS TO UPDATE A FEW OF THE COMPUTER SYSTEMS HERE AT THE CAVE.
THERE'S A LOT OF *HISTORY* HERE, ISN'T THERE?
YES. THIS IS WHERE IT ALL STARTED. WHEN THE JUSTICE LEAGUE WAS FIRST FORMED, THIS WAS THEIR BASE OF OPERATIONS.

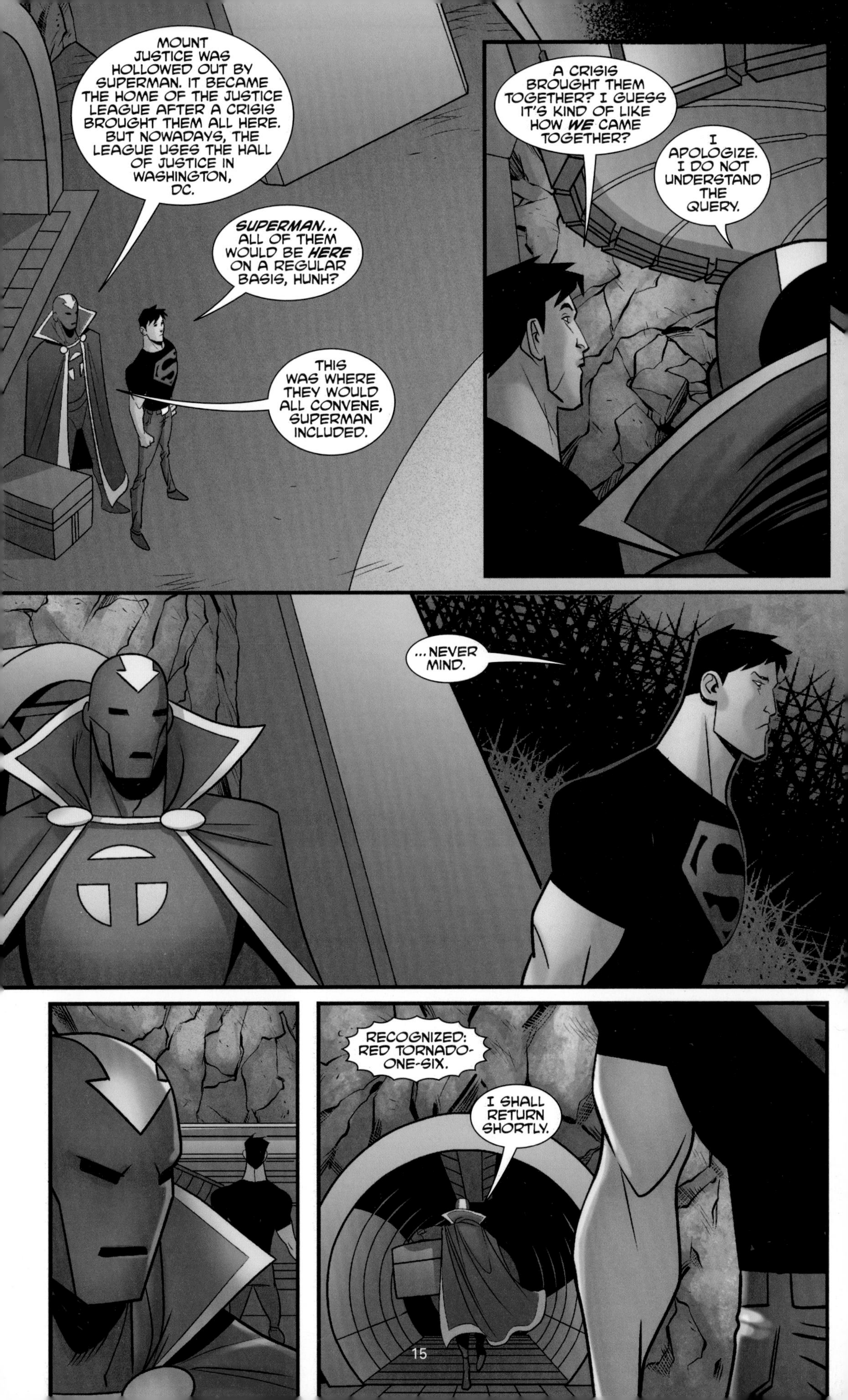
MOUNT JUSTICE WAS HOLLOWED OUT BY SUPERMAN. IT BECAME THE HOME OF THE JUSTICE LEAGUE AFTER A CRISIS BROUGHT THEM ALL HERE. BUT NOWADAYS, THE LEAGUE USES THE HALL OF JUSTICE IN WASHINGTON, DC.
SUPERMAN... ALL OF THEM WOULD BE HERE ON A REGULAR BASIS, HUNH?
THIS WAS WHERE THEY WOULD ALL CONVENE, SUPERMAN INCLUDED.
A CRISIS BROUGHT THEM TOGETHER? I GUESS IT'S KIND OF LIKE HOW WE CAME TOGETHER?
I APOLOGIZE. I DO NOT UNDERSTAND THE QUERY.
...NEVER MIND.
RECOGNIZED: RED TORNADO- ONE-SIX.
I SHALL RETURN SHORTLY.

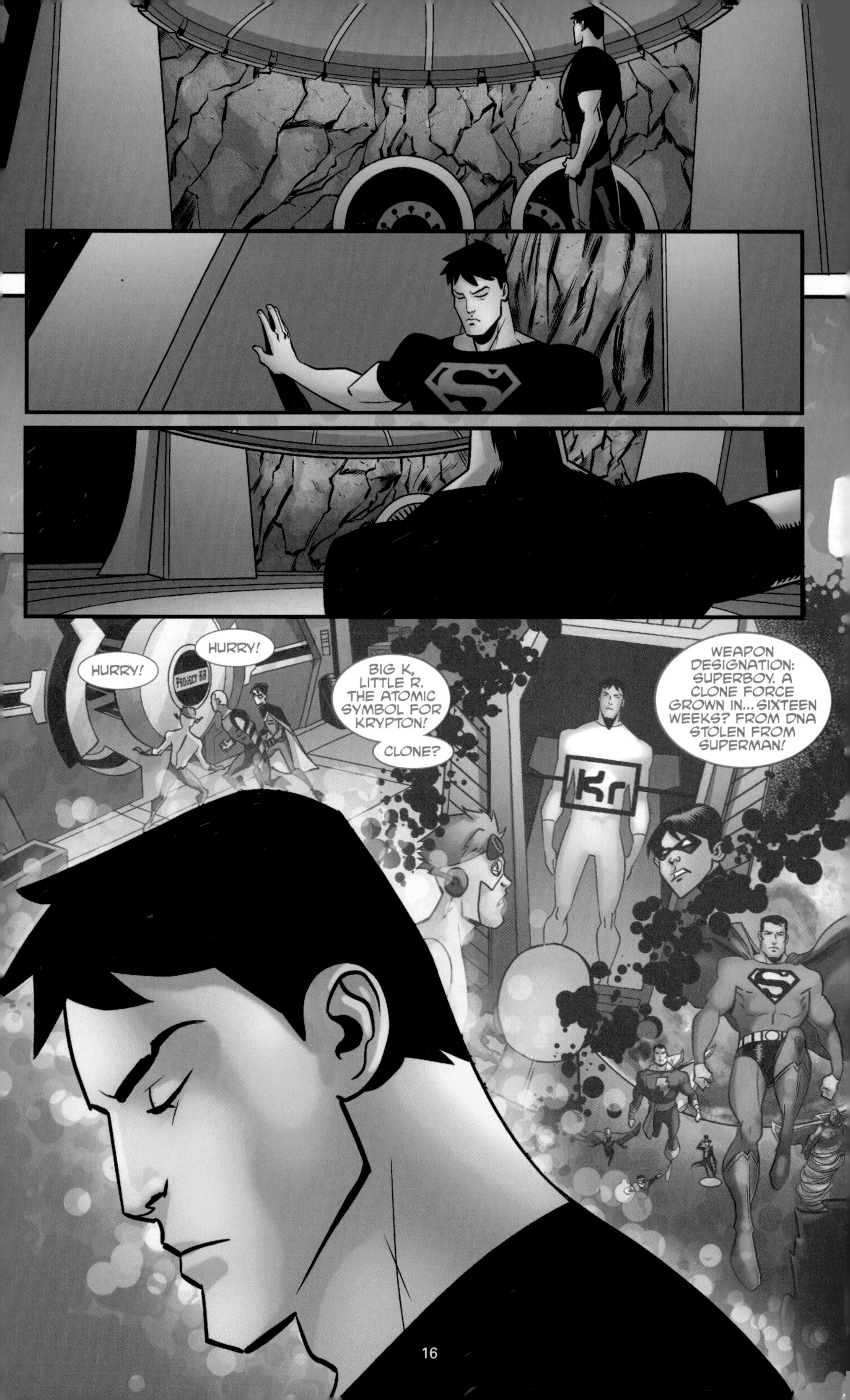
HURRY!
HURRY!
BIG K, LITTLE R. THE ATOMIC SYMBOL FOR KRYPTON!
CLONE?
WEAPON DESIGNATION: SUPERBOY. A CLONE FORCE GROWN IN... SIXTEEN WEEKS? FROM DNA STOLEN FROM SUPERMAN!

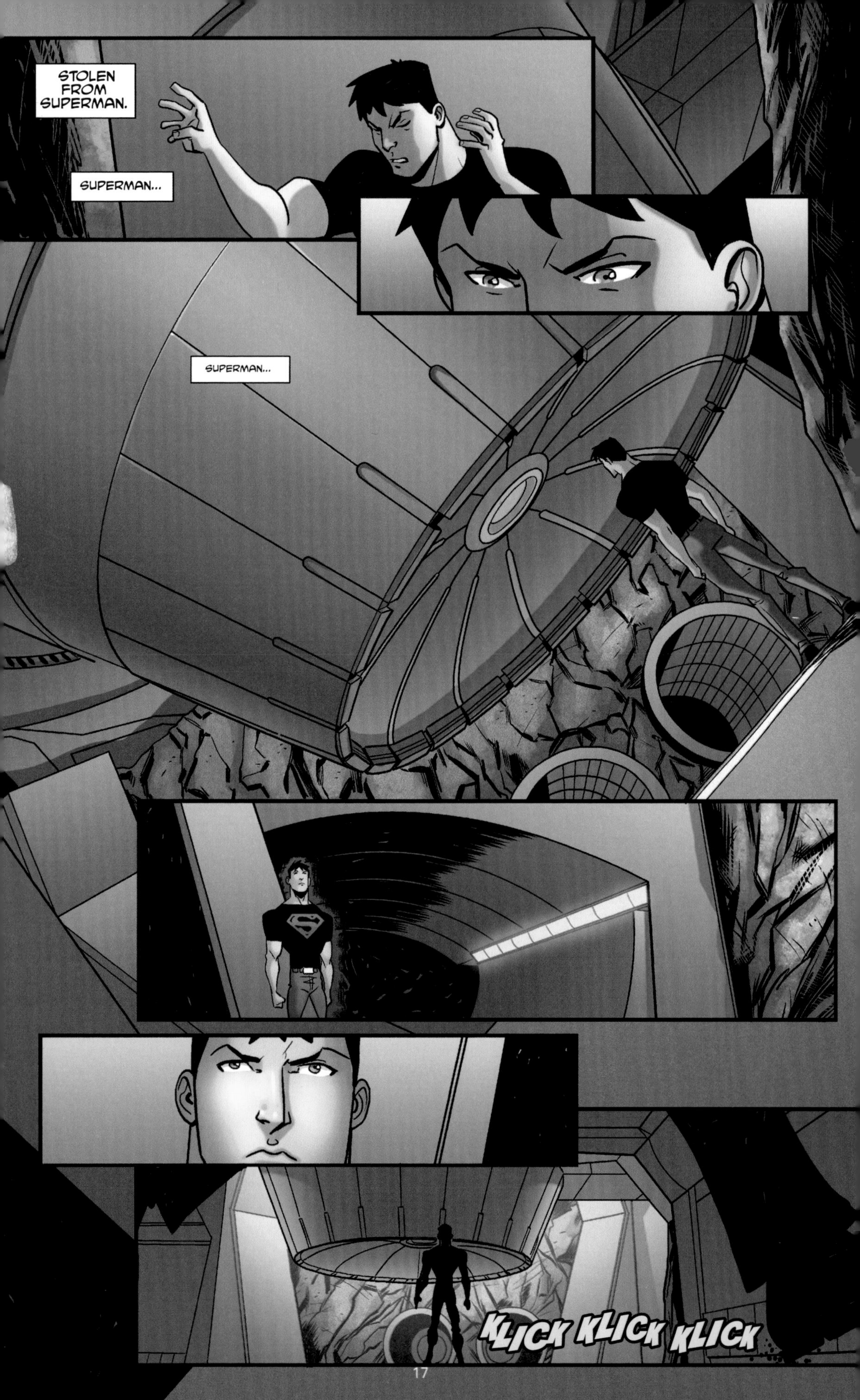

STOLEN FROM SUPERMAN.
SUPERMAN...
SUPERMAN...
KLICK KLICK KLICK

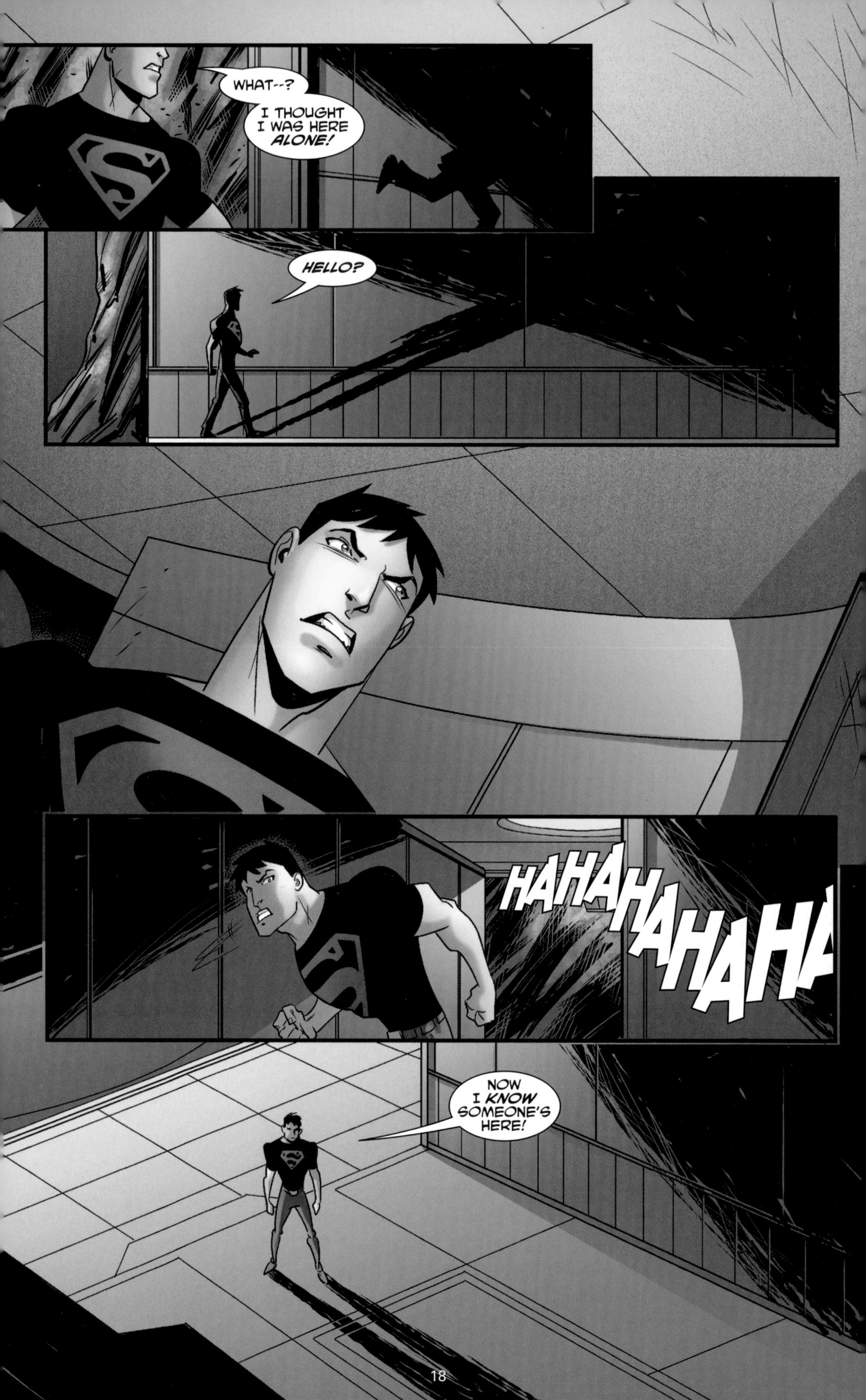
WHAT--?
I THOUGHT I WAS HERE *ALONE!*
HELLO?
HAHAHAHAHAHAHA
NOW I *KNOW* SOMEONE'S HERE!

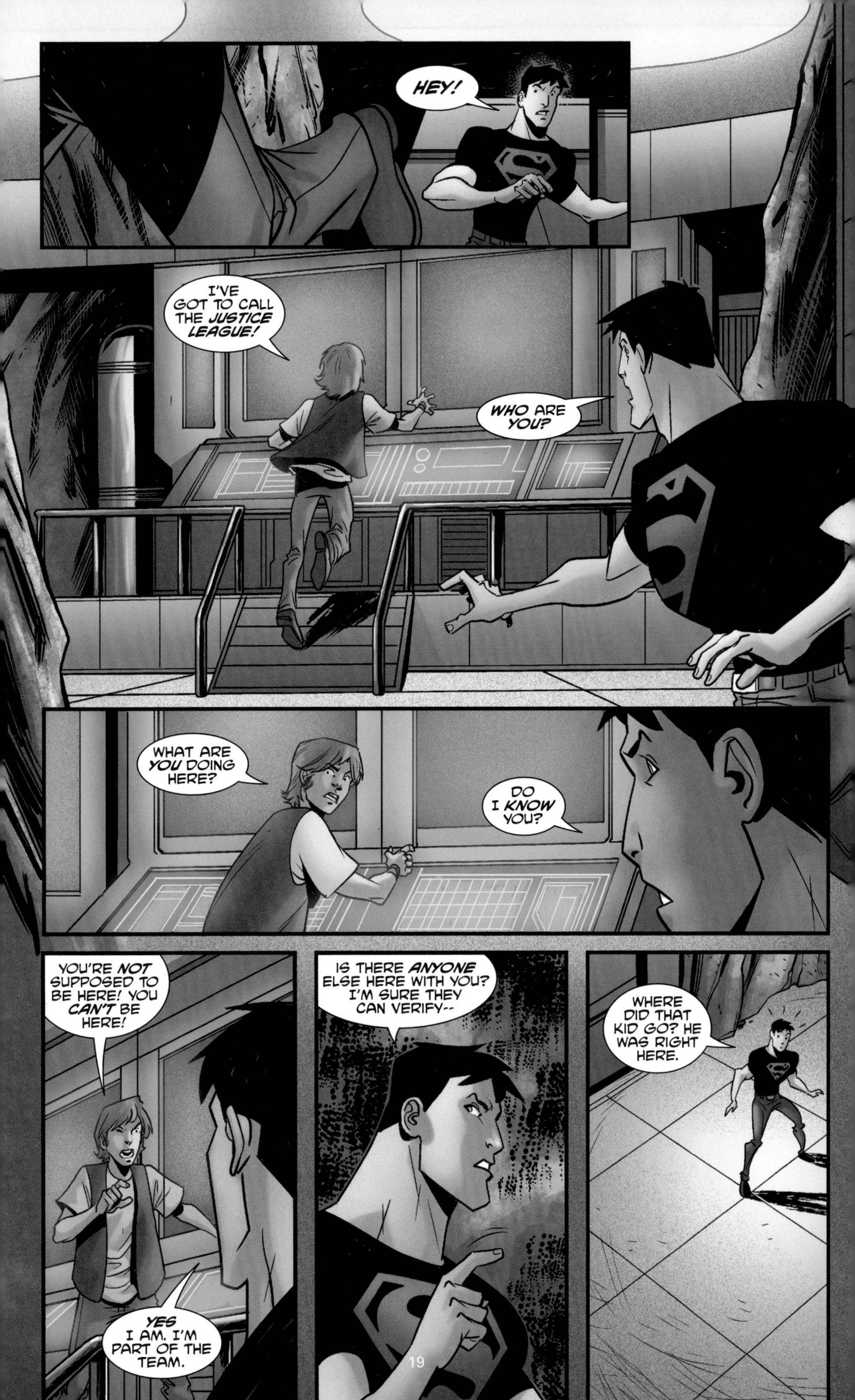
HEY!
I'VE GOT TO CALL THE JUSTICE LEAGUE!
WHO ARE YOU?
WHAT ARE YOU DOING HERE?
DO I KNOW YOU?
YOU'RE NOT SUPPOSED TO BE HERE! YOU CAN'T BE HERE!
YES I AM. I'M PART OF THE TEAM.
IS THERE ANYONE ELSE HERE WITH YOU? I'M SURE THEY CAN VERIFY--
WHERE DID THAT KID GO? HE WAS RIGHT HERE.

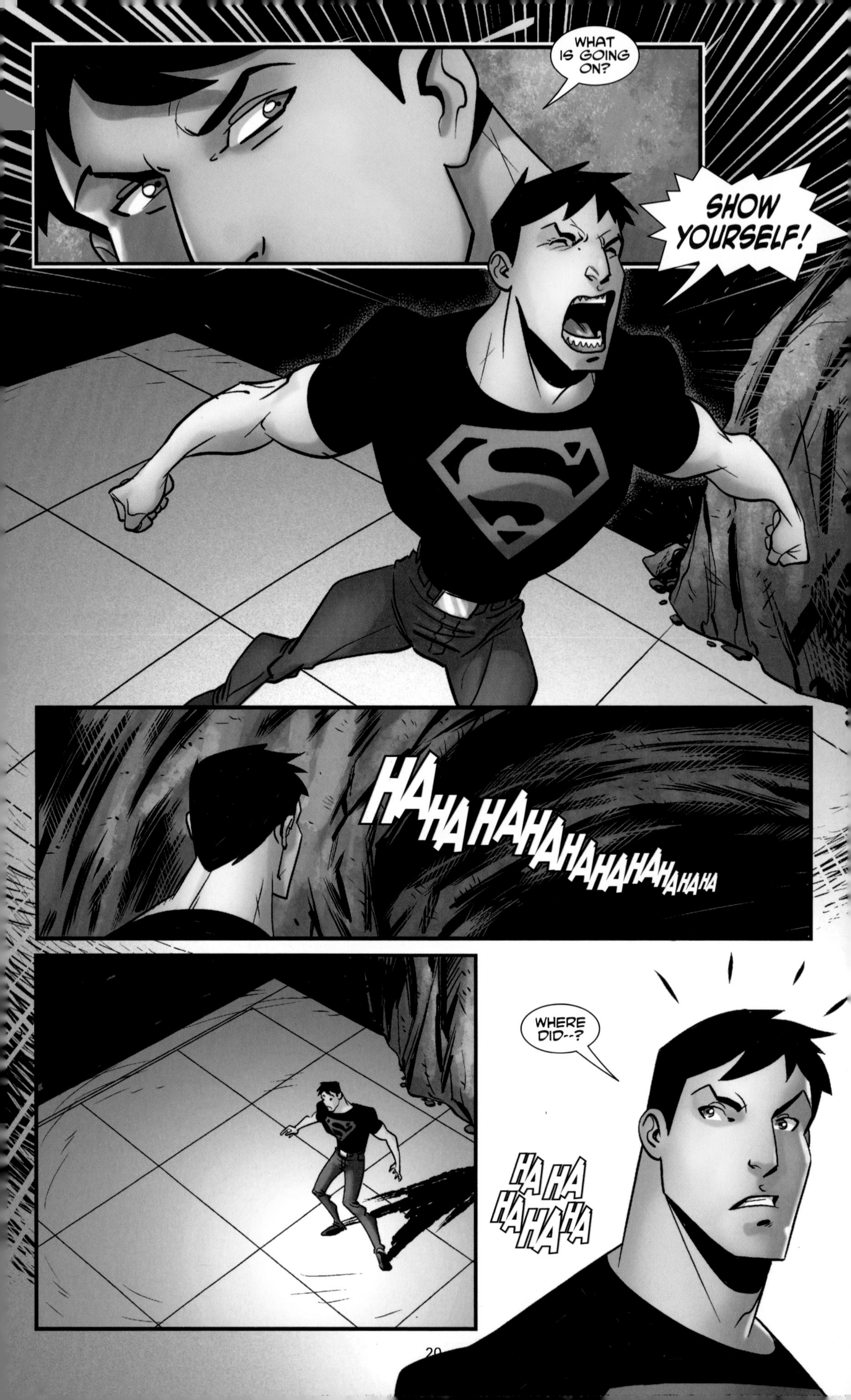
WHAT IS GOING ON?
SHOW YOURSELF!
HAHAHAHAHAHAHAHAHAHAHAHAHA
WHERE DID--?
HA HA HA HA HA HA

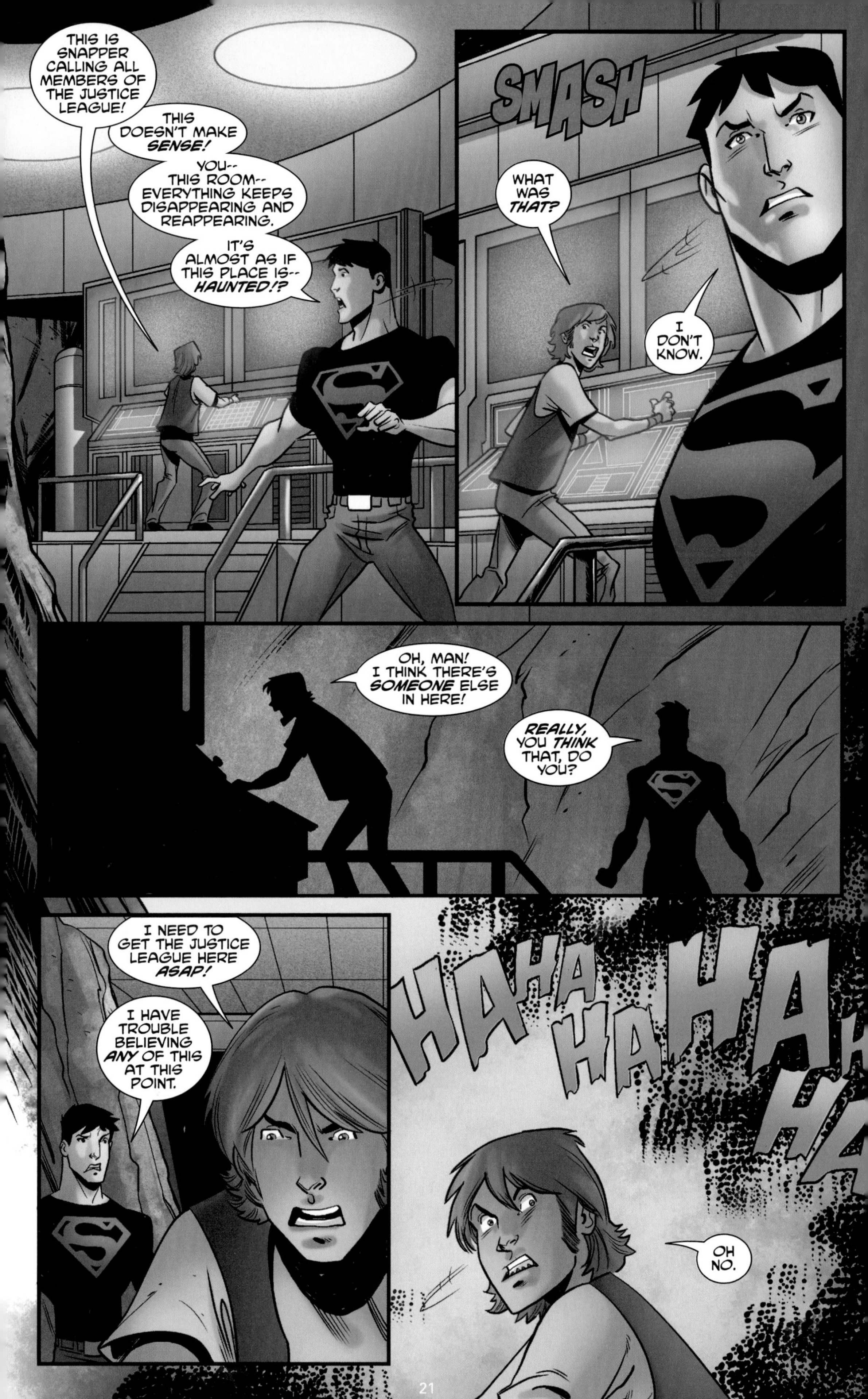
THIS IS SNAPPER CALLING ALL MEMBERS OF THE JUSTICE LEAGUE!
THIS DOESN'T MAKE SENSE!
YOU-- THIS ROOM-- EVERYTHING KEEPS DISAPPEARING AND REAPPEARING.
IT'S ALMOST AS IF THIS PLACE IS-- HAUNTED!?
SMASH
WHAT WAS THAT?
I DON'T KNOW.
OH, MAN! I THINK THERE'S SOMEONE ELSE IN HERE!
REALLY, YOU THINK THAT, DO YOU?
I NEED TO GET THE JUSTICE LEAGUE HERE ASAP!
I HAVE TROUBLE BELIEVING ANY OF THIS AT THIS POINT.
HAHA HAHA
OH NO.

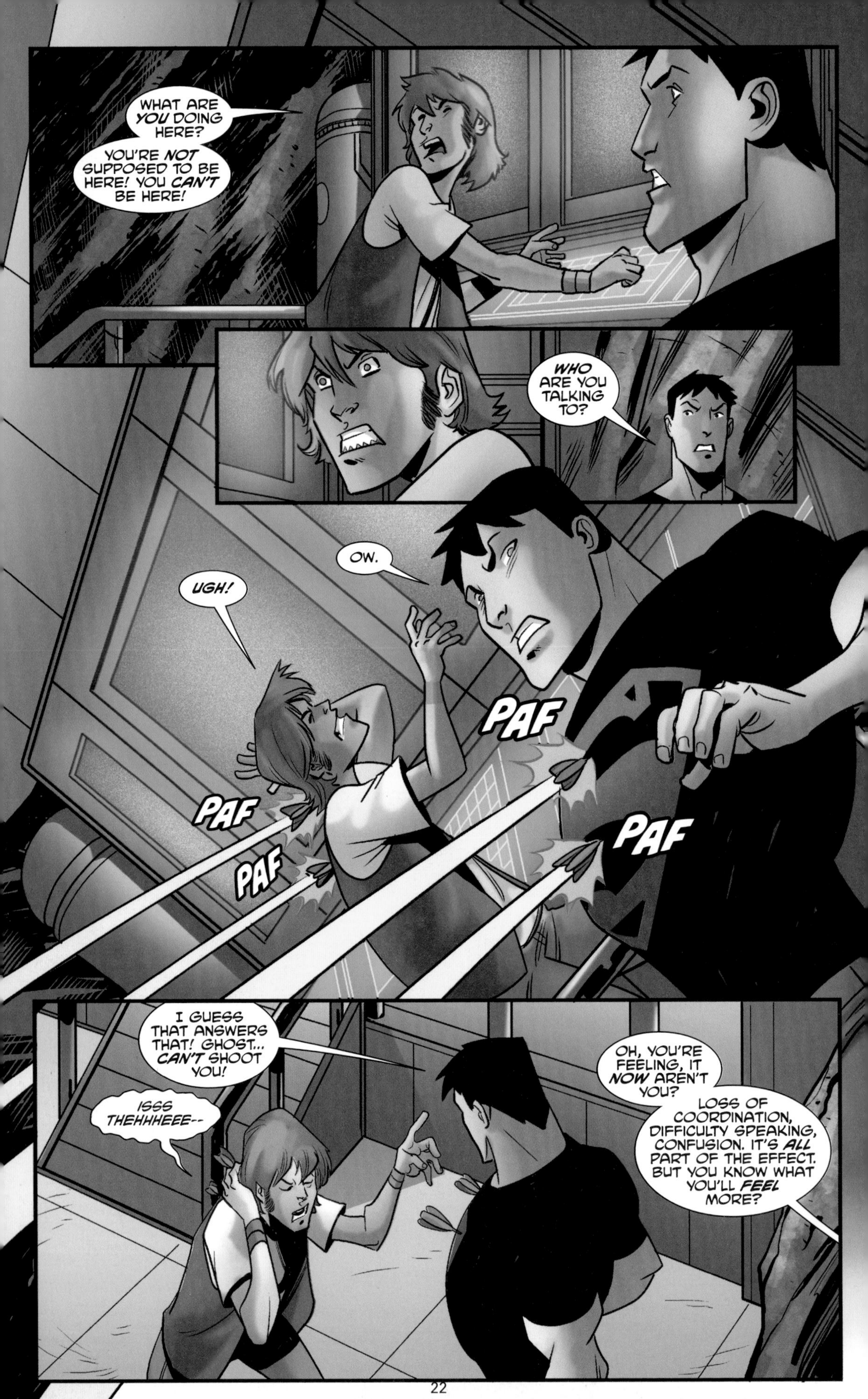
WHAT ARE YOU DOING HERE?
YOU'RE NOT SUPPOSED TO BE HERE! YOU CAN'T BE HERE!
WHO ARE YOU TALKING TO?
OW.
UGH!
PAF
PAF
PAF
PAF
I GUESS THAT ANSWERS THAT! GHOST... CAN'T SHOOT YOU!
ISSS THEHHHEEE--
OH, YOU'RE FEELING, IT NOW AREN'T YOU?
LOSS OF COORDINATION, DIFFICULTY SPEAKING, CONFUSION. IT'S ALL PART OF THE EFFECT. BUT YOU KNOW WHAT YOU'LL FEEL MORE?

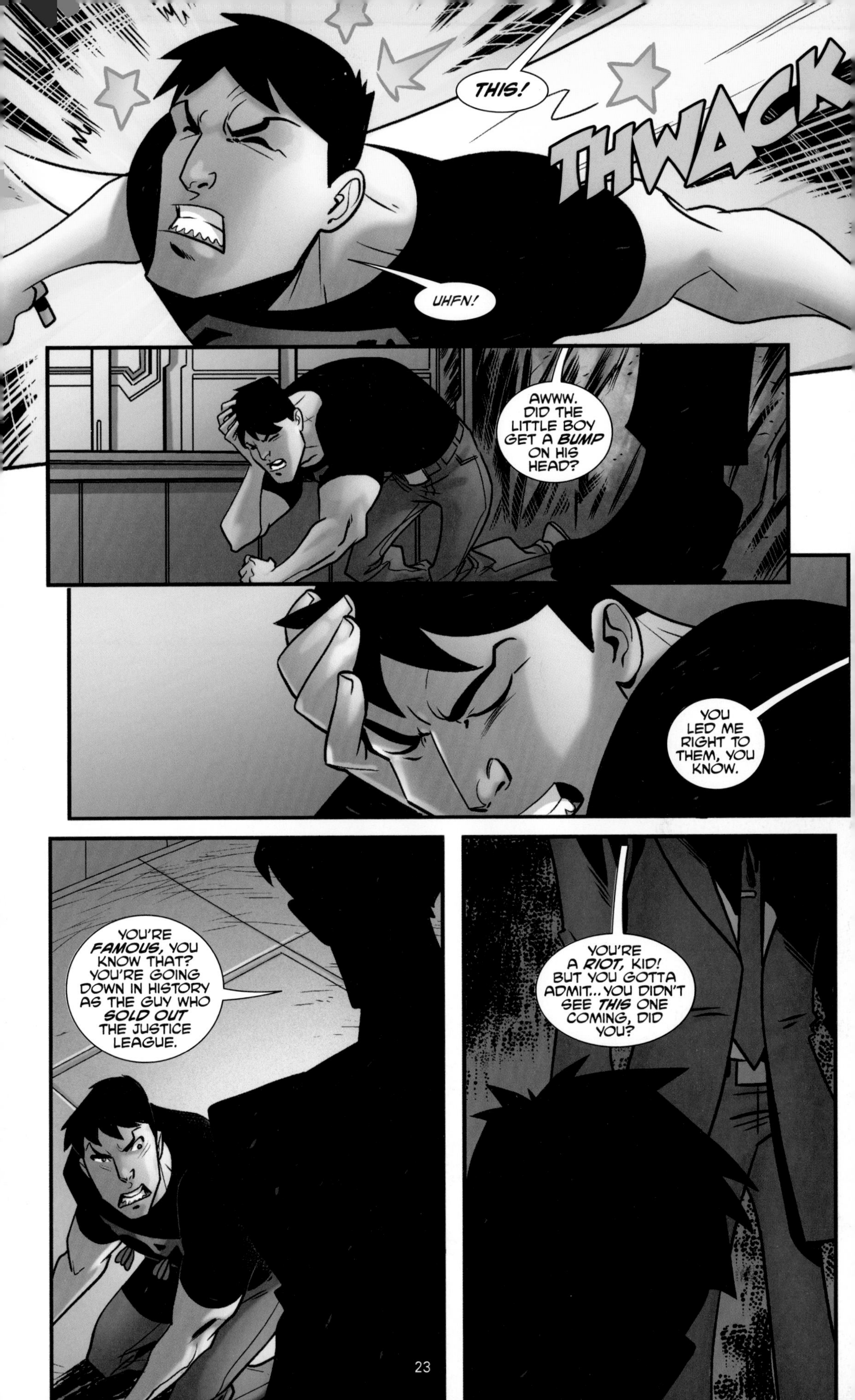
THIS!
THWACK
UHFN!
AWWW. DID THE LITTLE BOY GET A BUMP ON HIS HEAD?
YOU LED ME RIGHT TO THEM, YOU KNOW.
YOU'RE FAMOUS, YOU KNOW THAT? YOU'RE GOING DOWN IN HISTORY AS THE GUY WHO SOLD OUT THE JUSTICE LEAGUE.
YOU'RE A RIOT, KID! BUT YOU GOTTA ADMIT... YOU DIDN'T SEE THIS ONE COMING, DID YOU?

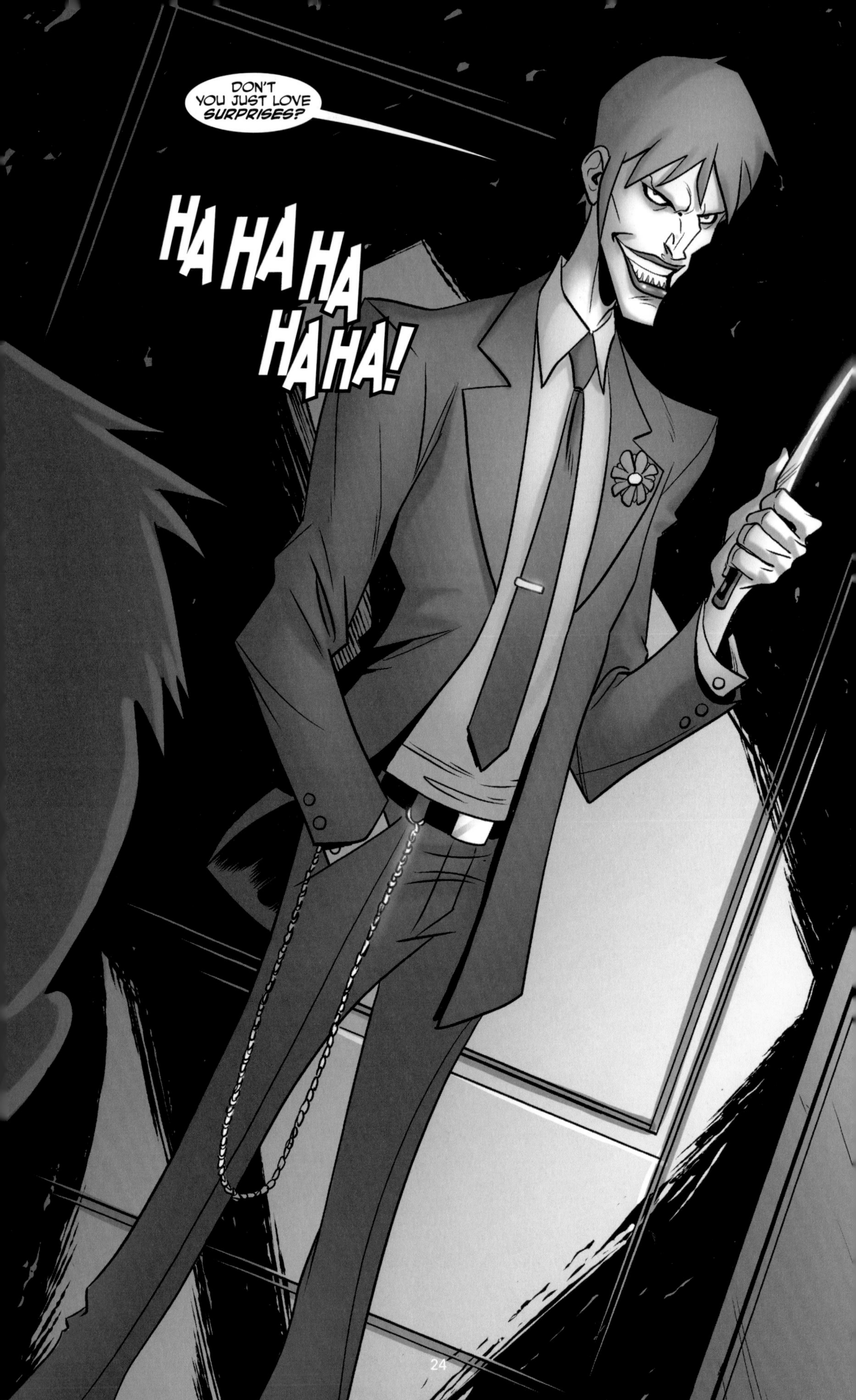
DON'T YOU JUST LOVE SURPRISES?
HA HA HA HA
HA HA!

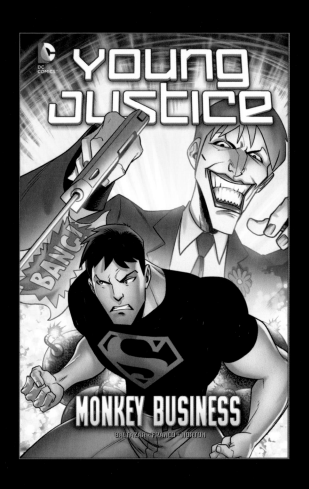

CREATORS

ART BALTAZAR WRITER

Art Baltazar is a cartoonist machine from the heart of Chicago! He defines cartoons and comics not only as an art style, but as a way of life. Currently, Art is the creative force behind *The New York Times* best-selling, Eisner Award-winning, DC Comics series Tiny Titans, and the co-writer for Billy Batson and the Magic of SHAZAM! and co-creator of Superman Family Adventures. Art is living the dream! He draws comics and never has to leave the house. He lives with his lovely wife, Rose, big boy Sonny, little boy Gordon, and little girl Audrey. Right on!

FRANCO AURELIANI WRITER

Bronx, New York born writer and artist Franco Aureliani has been drawing comics since he could hold a crayon. Currently residing in upstate New York with his wife, Ivette, and son, Nicolas, Franco spends most of his days in a Batcave-like studio where he produces DC's Tiny Titans comics. In 1995, Franco founded Blindwolf Studios, an independent art studio where he and fellow creators can create children's comics. Franco is the creator, artist, and writer of Weirdsville, L'il Creeps, and Eagle All Star, as well as the co-creator and writer of Patrick the Wolf Boy. When he's not writing and drawing, Franco also teaches high school art.

MIKE NORTON ARTIST

Mike Norton has been a professional comic book artist for more than ten years. His best-known works for DC Comics include the series Young Justice, All-New Atom, and Green Arrow/Black Canary.

GLOSSARY

crisis (KRYE-siss)--a time of danger and difficulty

designation (dez-ig-NAY-shuhn)--a name or label for someone or something

encrypted (en-KRIPT-id)--encoded or written in a way that makes a message secure

familiarize (fuh-MIL-yur-ize)--if you familiarize yourself with something, you get to know it very well

gig (GIG)--a special event or activity

honored (ON-urd)--gave praise or an award

potential (puh-TEN-shuhl)--your potential is what you are capable of doing

query (KWEER-ee)--to ask a question

recognized (REK-ugh-nized)--saw someone and knew who that person was

verify (VER-uh-fye)--prove that something is true

VISUAL QUESTIONS & PROMPTS

1. Which super hero do you think Kid Flash is talking about here?

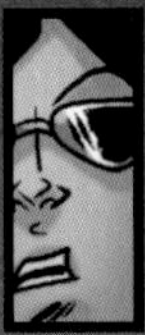

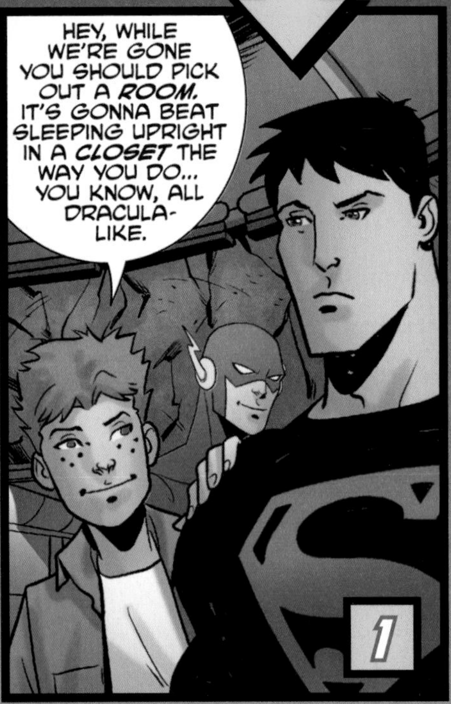
HEY, WHILE WE'RE GONE YOU SHOULD PICK OUT A *ROOM.* IT'S GONNA BEAT SLEEPING UPRIGHT IN A *CLOSET* THE WAY YOU DO... YOU KNOW, ALL DRACULA-LIKE.
1

2. What do you think is in these darts? Explain your answer.

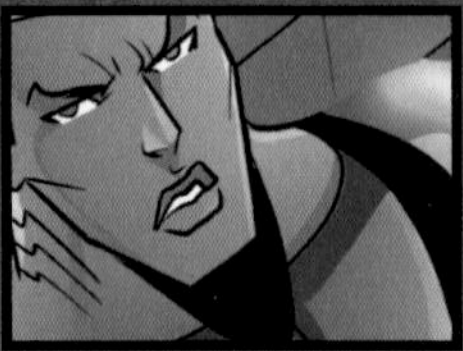

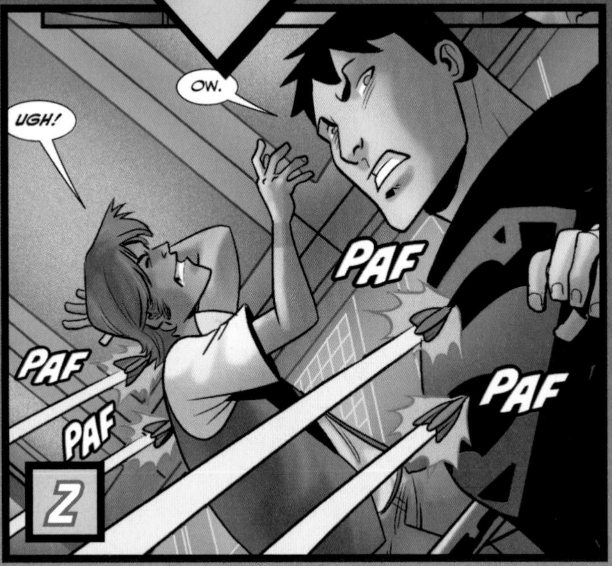
OW.
UGH!
PAF
PAF
PAF
PAF
2

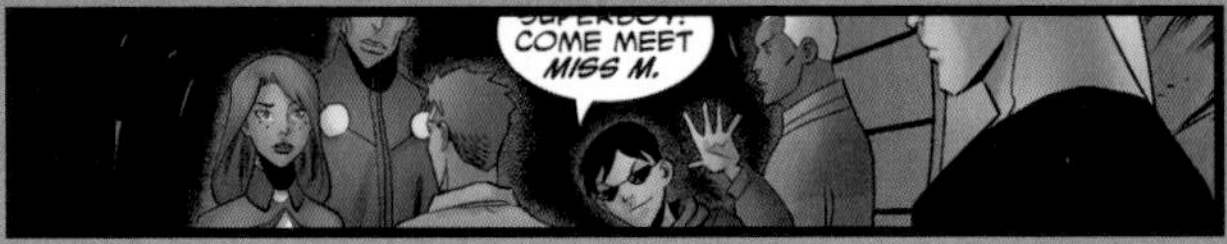
COME MEET MISS M.

3. Based on this two-panel sequence, why do you think Miss Martian copied Superboy's t-shirt design? Explain yourself, using specific panels to support your claim.

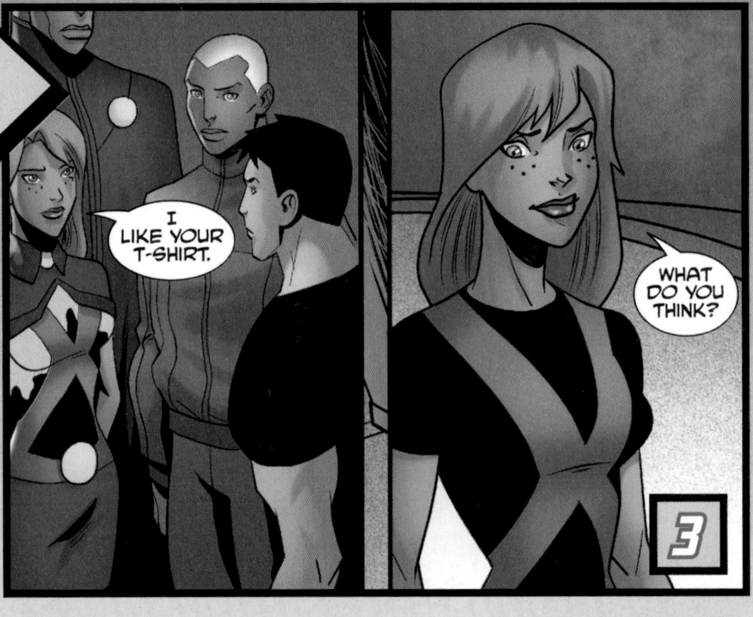
I LIKE YOUR T-SHIRT.
WHAT DO YOU THINK?
3

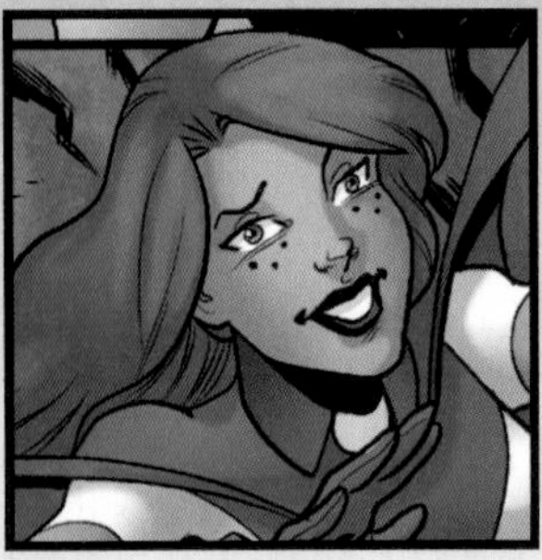

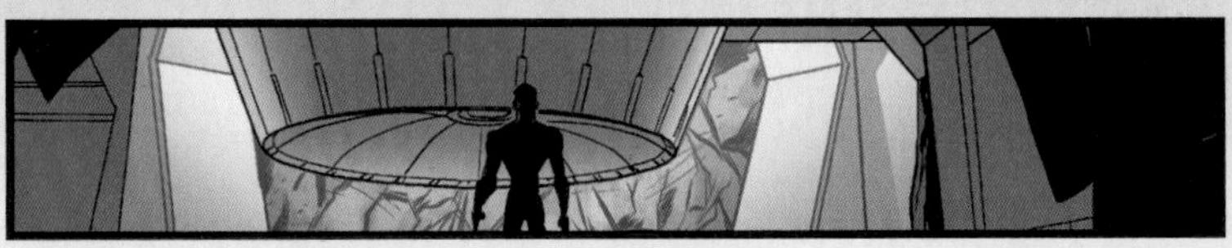

4. What do you think this room is? Why does Superboy want it for himself?

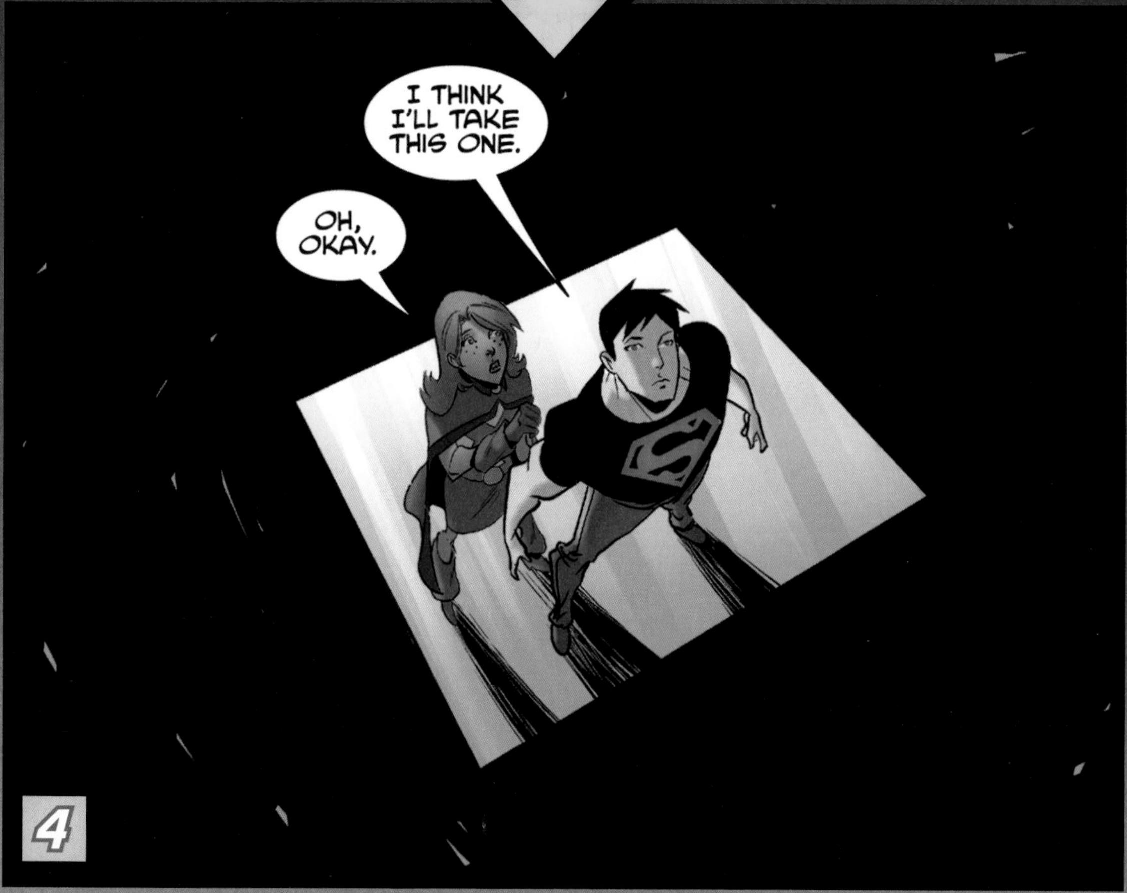
I THINK I'LL TAKE THIS ONE.
OH, OKAY.
4

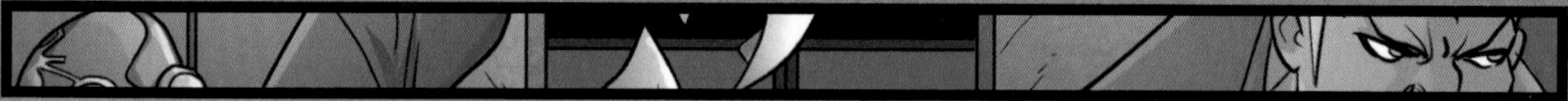

5. What do you think is happening in these panels? Is Superboy imagining those events? Why or why not?

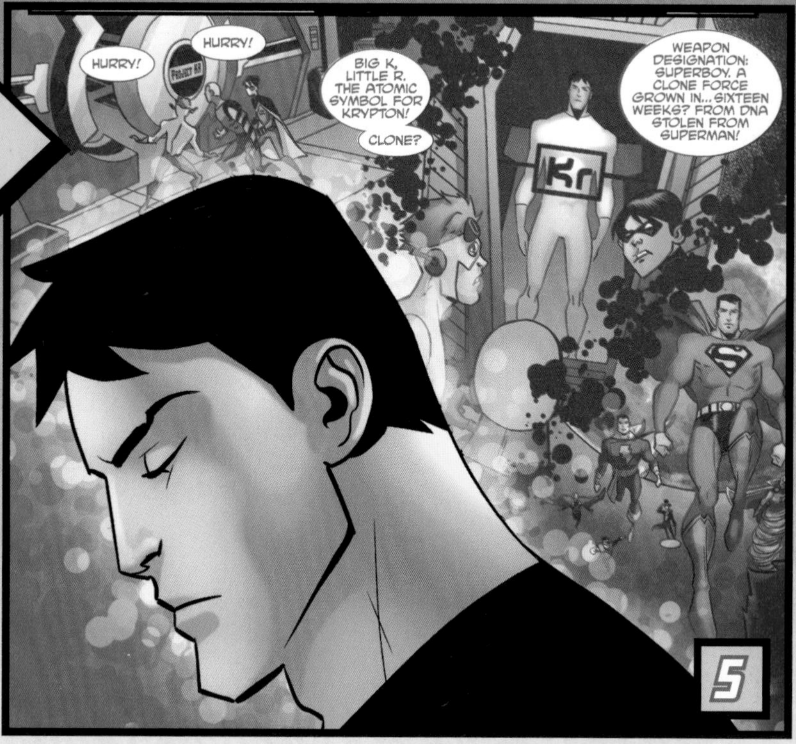
HURRY!
HURRY!
BIG K, LITTLE R. THE ATOMIC SYMBOL FOR KRYPTON!
CLONE?
WEAPON DESIGNATION: SUPERBOY. A CLONE FORCE GROWN IN... SIXTEEN WEEKS? FROM DNA STOLEN FROM SUPERMAN!
Kr
5

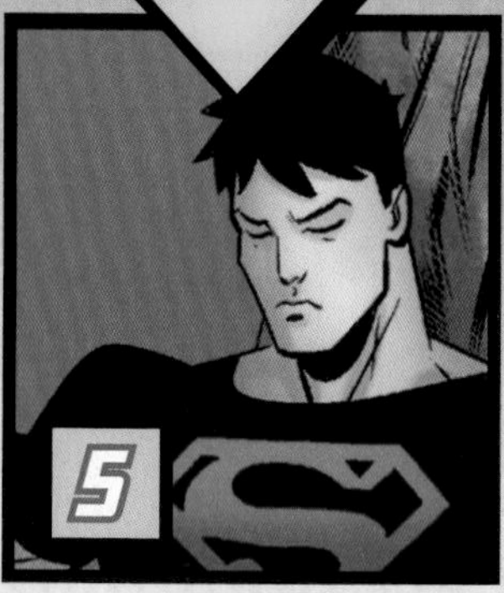
5

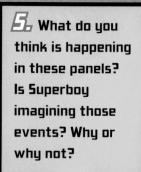

young justice ™